Little Arliss

Other Books by Fred Gipson

LITTLE
ARLISS

by **FRED GIPSON**
Illustrations by **RONALD HIMLER**

HARPER & ROW, PUBLISHERS
New York, Hagerstown, San Francisco, London

LITTLE ARLISS

Text copyright © 1978 by Thomas Beckton Gipson
Illustrations copyright © 1978 by Ronald Himler

First Edition

Library of Congress Cataloging in Publication Data
Gipson, Frederick Benjamin, 1908–1973
    Little Arliss.

    SUMMARY: A small twelve-year-old boy's determination
to prove he is tough sets him on the trail of a runaway
horse.
    [1. Horses—Fiction.   2. Western stories]
I. Himler, Ronald.   II. Title.
PZ7.G4393Li   [Fic]   77–17643
ISBN 0–06–022008–2
ISBN 0–06–022009–0 lib. bdg.

To Ben and Tom Gipson

CONTENTS

One

NOBODY with a teaspoonful of brains between his ears would ever have gotten mixed up with that old scalawag horse in the first place. I know I wouldn't have if I'd ever taken time off to think. But I was too mad to think. They had been picking on me for too long. All I wanted to do was fight back.

It was Papa and Mama and my grown-up brother Travis and Burn Sanderson and just about anybody else around the Salt Licks settlement that you could lay name to. They were every one to blame. From as far back as I could recollect they had all called me *Little* Arliss and stood in the way of my doing anything worthwhile by yelling, "Arliss! You can't do that. You're too little."

Well, a body can stand just so much. After that he gets as touchy as a nest of yellow jackets. Tamper with him the least little bit and he's done swarming all over you.

That's about the frame of mind I was in the

morning my troubles with that old outlaw horse started taking shape.

I was in the kitchen part of our log cabin, all swelled up like a pestered horned frog. This was because Mama had me soaping my neck and ears for a second go-around, claiming that all I'd done with my first washing was start the dirt to running.

"And you hurry up," she went on. "I don't want to hear tell of your getting late to school again."

That touched another one of my sore spots. "School! School!" I moaned. "That's all I hear, for three whole months out of every year. Reading and writing and figuring, all day long. Then come home at night to bake my eyeballs out against the lamplight, trying to stuff my head with more learning. It's enough to drive a body crazy!"

Mama didn't show much bother. She lifted a pot of hot water from the fireplace and poured it into her dishpan. Then she said, "Well, it's enough to drive me crazy, having to drive you to school every day."

About then is when my old trailhound, Savage Sam, started a big uproar outside.

I threw down my washrag and made a run for the door.

"Arliss!" Mama called. "You come back here, young man."

"Just want to see who's coming," I said, and kept going.

[4]

I ran out to stand in the dog run that separated the two rooms of our cabin. From there I could look down the slope to where the road from Salt Licks crossed Birdsong Creek.

A party of riders was splashing their horses across the creek and moving in under the tall trees that grew beside the water.

Savage Sam, all stove up with age and too many bobcat fights, went crippling off down the slant. He had his hackles raised and was baying the riders like they were hog-catching panthers.

"It's Mr. Sanderson," I called back to Mama. "And Travis and old man Searcy and Wiley Crouch."

Mama came to stare out the kitchen door. Papa rounded the corner of the cabin and yelled at Sam.

"Sam!" he fussed. "You hush up that racket."

Sam paid no mind to Papa.

The party came toward the cabin, riding single file, Indian fashion. I took note of each one while we waited for them to come within talking distance.

Sanderson rode in the lead. He was a big tall man with a wide warm grin. Sometimes he man-hunted with the Texas Rangers, but mostly he looked after a cow-and-horse ranch he had built up over on Little Devil's River. He was my friend and the finest neighbor a body could have.

My brother came next. Travis wasn't nearly as

[5]

big as Sanderson, but he sat a horse like I wished I could. Sanderson had taken him in as a ranch partner, but I didn't know why. Travis would work, all right—or always had. Until the fall before when he and Searcy's granddaughter Lisbeth had thrown up a cabin at Bull Head Springs and planted a couple of graveyard cedars out front. Since then they had been so busy being married I didn't see how Travis ever got around to doing anything else.

Behind Travis rode Searcy. He was an old blowhard, born with a potbelly, a flappy jaw, and an appetite to shame a hog. He would lie when the truth was easier, but his lies were mostly of a kind to hurt nobody. I couldn't much help liking the grizzly old coot.

Wiley Crouch though, the tail-end rider—a body would have to put in a whole lot of time at hard thinking to find anything good to say about him. He was a stringy, soured-out buffalo hunter. He wore a face as ugly as anything you're apt to meet outside of a jail. He was cantankerous as a javelina hog, and I wouldn't have trusted him out of sight with a pair of frazzled-out suspenders.

I wondered what they were doing out so early. I sure hoped it was something to save me from school.

Sam finally caught their scent and recognized them as neighbors. Then he changed his baying to

Won't take me but a minute to saddle up."

I tore out in a run toward the corral but got stopped before I'd made twenty tracks.

"Arliss!" Papa hollered at me.

I had a sinking spell when I turned to face him. I had a pretty good idea what was coming next.

"Who said you could go?" Papa wanted to know.

"Who said I couldn't?" I bristled up. "I can be as much help as anybody."

Papa was slow to answer, like maybe what I'd said was worth thinking about. Then old man Searcy had to spill a bunch of his drivel.

"Why, boy," he said. "That Onion Creek country, it's rough. Ain't no place for a little old knothead youngun to be chasing bad horses."

That made me mad all over. That was the sort of thing I'd done heard too many times. "You keep your big lip out of this," I told Searcy.

"Arliss!" Papa's voice was full of threat. "You watch how you speak to a grown man."

Sometimes a body's mouth gets to running off from his brains. I knew better than to say what I said next, but I was too riled to hold it.

"Well," I said, "I can ride a horse anywhere that old tub of leaf lard can go!"

Searcy's mouth fell open. He looked around, his eyes full of surprise and hurt. Papa reached for a braided rawhide quirt hanging to Sanderson's saddle. Grinning, Sanderson caught and held the quirt.

"Look, Arliss," Sanderson began in a voice so full of reason that it just burned me down. You can bet your last marble that any time a grown-up starts being reasonable, you're done licked. I didn't even let him finish.

"I know!" I said. "I'm too *little* to go. I'm always too little. For anything besides corn-hoeing or hog-slopping or chopping firewood."

"Now, Arliss, I didn't say that," Sanderson said.

I could feel my tear bucket fixing to slop over, which made me madder than ever.

"You don't have to," I yelled at him. "You've done said it. You've all said it. A thousand times!"

By now I was wound up tighter than an eight-day clock. I pointed a finger at Sanderson. "You said it last month when I offered to help you track down them horse thieves." I swung on Papa and told him. "You said it when I wanted to join up with that trail drive to Kansas last spring." I wheeled around to take in Travis. "You said it when I wanted to help break out that string of Brad Tully horses. And Mama," I said, turning to her, "she won't let me ride nothing to school that's fit to run a horse race on."

I took a big deep breath. "Now," I said, "I'm getting a bellyful of being told I ain't big enough for nothing. I'm maybe not as big as some twelve-year-olds, but I'll tell you one thing, I'm a whole heap tougher!"

Brimful of mad, I looked around, just daring anybody to argue.

The men didn't. They every one knew I was telling the gospel truth. They just stood and stared at me and at each other.

Then Mama had to go spoil it. She laughed. Right out loud. "Well, Toughy," she said, "you're still not going off on this horse hunt. You're going to school. You're going to get an education."

I turned on Mama like a biting dog. *"Education!"* I screamed. "Why confound it, I'm done educated clear out of all reason!"

That's when they *all* laughed at me. Mama and Papa and Burn Sanderson—slapping his leg and whooping—and Travis, looking all grown up and smug with schooling—and even old man Searcy and Wiley Crouch, neither one of which had any more book-learning than a spotted civet cat.

Well, that did it. I blew sky high. I bent and started grabbing up rocks off the ground. I went to throwing them as hard as I could.

"Laugh!" I yelled at them. "I'll learn you who to laugh at."

I did, too. In half a second I had them scattering like flushed quail, ducking and dodging and hollering.

Then a rock missed Travis and cracked against the jawbone of Wiley Crouch's little Coon horse. He snorted and reared. He fell back against the bridle reins, ripping the top rail off the yard fence. And Savage Sam, he kept the excitement going by baying at the top of his voice and snapping at the horses' heels.

Then out of the noisy scramble came Papa. He had Burn Sanderson's quirt gripped in one hand. His face was as black as a big storm cloud.

"Arliss!" he was hollering at me. "Drop them rocks. You hear! Right now. And come here to me!"

Well, I dropped the rocks. Just like he said. But I sure wasn't fool enough to come there. Not with him wearing that look on his face. Riled up like Papa was now, he aimed to set the seat of my pants to smoking.

I turned tail. I broke and ran for it. I tore out toward the creek-crossing, running like a scalded dog. Headed for school, which I hated, because it was the only safe place to go. Going afoot because there was no time to saddle my old gray mare, Nellie. Running—and bawling my head off.

Dang 'em, they'd whipped me out again!

Two

───

SOME days a body just naturally gets a threadbare run of luck. This was one of those days. It started out bad, and trouble kept piling up.

To begin with, having to walk all that far, I got late to school. So, of course, old Hoot Owl Weatherby, our schoolmaster, gave me the treatment. He pulled his glasses down on his nose till he could stare over them with his big round hoot-owl eyes.

He had hoot-owl tuffs of scraggly hair standing above each ear. He had a hoot-owl beak, a hoot-owl figure, and a hoot-owl way of getting mad and puffing up his feathers. But it was his yellow-eyed hoot-owl stare that was the worst. It could just wither you.

It withered me.

He didn't say anything. He just stared. He started his stare when I came through the door. He kept on staring while I walked down the aisle to my desk. He was still staring when I sat down, and he kept right on at it till he had every kid in the room staring, too.

He knew what he was doing. He knew that if he kept up his treatment long enough, he'd have me feeling as low and squirmy as a worm under a rock.

Well, I got the feeling, all right. But this morning, after that round at home, I'd come in with my fur raised. So I braced myself and matched him, stare for stare, looking him right in the eye.

It didn't save me, though. When he saw that he couldn't whittle me down, he smiled a nasty-nice smile and said in a nasty-nice voice, "We all regret, Arliss Coates, that you were detained this morning by matters much more important, no doubt, than our arithmetic class, but we'll still give you the opportunity to recite your multiplication tables."

Well, the switch was too quick for me. It threw me off. I made it up to eight-times-nine, then bogged clear down.

Hoot Owl waited, giving me plenty of time to look stupid. Then he sniffed like maybe I smelled bad and called on Illa Pratt.

Illa always had been a smarty-pants. Naturally, she could rattle off the tables like eating stick candy.

Next we took up spelling. Of course, the first one old Hoot Owl called on was me. The word was *rebellious*, but by this time, my wits were all wool.

[15]

Hoot Owl let me worry the word around till I was all hot under the collar, then said, in a snappy voice, "Young man, it is perfectly obvious that you have not studied your lessons for today."

"I have, too," I said. "I studied all last night. Mama seen to that."

"Seen!" Hoot Owl jumped like he'd been jabbed with a stick. "The word is *saw*."

"What?" I said. He had me puzzled.

"You do not say, 'Mama *seen* to that,' " he yelled at me. "You say, 'Mama *saw* to that.' "

I never did have any patience with picky people. "Well, all right," I said. "Seen or saw. It's all the same difference. Mama done it."

"*Done* it!" he screamed.

His face swelled up, red as a gobbler's snout. He gasped. He walled his eyeballs. He fought for air. For a second, it looked like he was bound to choke.

Then he groaned and shook his head and went on talking to himself. "Grammar! How can you teach it to the hoodlum offspring of a frontier community that doesn't even know it exists?"

His face took on the look of somebody whose folks have all gone off and died.

"The only mainstay of any language," he went on. "The only hope for clarity of expression and preciseness of communication. And they butcher it. They mangle it. They tear it to shreds."

[16]

It sure sounded hopeless, all right, the way he put it.

He went on for at least another five minutes, just talking to the overhead rafters, the best I could tell.

I wished Mama could have heard him. I just wished she could have seen how an overload of education can warp and twist a body's mind till their thinking runs clear off the track. It's a sort of sad thing to see.

All of a sudden, Hoot Owl hushed and pointed a ruler at me, squinting down it, like he was aiming a rifle.

"Arliss Coates!" he yelled. "Don't you ever *think*?"

I didn't like it, the way he aimed that ruler at me. I bristled up. "Think," I said. "Mama didn't tell me to think. She just kept pestering me to study. Till my eyeballs got to hanging out."

"Well, I'm telling you to think," he said. "I'm telling you to get after those lessons. Right now. And while you study, you *think*."

"Yes, sir!" I said.

So I sat down and opened my books and went to studying. And while I studied, I thought:

Bet Papa's sure going to tear my tail up this evening when I get home. If Sanderson don't talk him out of it. Sanderson will try; but can he do it?

Why wouldn't they let me go? Them all off, having a big time chasing a loose horse. And here I sit, thinking.

Why do they all have to keep picking on me? I ain't done nothing.

They're just trying to make me feel little. That's what.

I sat and I studied and I thought hard all morning. By dinnertime, when old Hoot Owl turned us all out to eat, I was feeling so sorry for myself that I couldn't hold it. I just *had* to tell somebody. So I followed Tim Utterback out to the shade tree that he generally ate under.

Scab Haley was a better friend to talk to. But leaving home in such a hurry that morning, I didn't have any lunch and had to eat with somebody. And I couldn't eat with Scab. I had done learned from experience what a complete ruin Scab's mama made of her cooking. It looked like she just worked at spoiling good grub. So I teamed up with Tim and told him my troubles.

"It ain't fair," I told him in a weepy voice. "It don't make sense. I can throw a rock harder and straighter than anybody I know. I can dive deeper and swim farther. I can run faster. I can shoot a rifle with the best of them. I can ride anybody's old pitching milk calf right down to a whisper. I can fist-whip any boy in school. But none of it don't

[18]

make no difference. They won't let me do nothing. They keep claiming I'm too little."

I thought Tim had brains enough to understand what I was talking about, but he didn't. All he wanted to do was argue.

He stopped eating long enough to give me a careful sizing-up, then said, "You ain't never fist-whupped me."

" 'Course not," I said. "Ain't never had no call to. We always been friends."

"Well, we ain't friends no more," he said.

I looked at him in surprise. "How come we ain't friends no more?" I asked.

"I ain't friends with nobody," he said; "and them going around bragging how they can fist-whup me."

I began to swell up. "Dang it!" I said, "I ain't bragging. All I'm trying to do is tell how nobody won't let me do nothing I want to."

He snorted and sneered at me. "Well, it sounds like bragging to me."

I thought anybody that stupid ought to be hit in the face with a butter-and-jelly biscuit, so that's what I did. Then we both jumped to our feet and started mixing it, hot and fast.

Well, at the start, Tim managed to land a couple of lucky licks. One split my lip; the other blooded my nose. But that was before I got going good.

After that, a blind man could see how this fight was going to turn out. I was fixing to wipe up the earth with Tim Utterback.

I'd have done it, too, if it hadn't been for Clara Todd.

Clara was a little bitty thing. She was pesky as most females but not nasty-mean or smarty-pants like some. Not like Illa Pratt. And I sure didn't go to hurt her, like I did. The thing is, I didn't see her. All I saw was that big haymaker Tim swung at me. He'd reached back and brought it up off the ground, and I knew if it landed it would knock my head clean off my shoulders. So I outsmarted him and ran backwards. And little Clara, she was right behind me, hollering with excitement, like all the rest of the kids crowding the fight. And I ran over her and knocked her flat on her back, then trampled on her, trying to get off.

Well, of course, Clara screamed. What else could you expect? And all the other girls screamed louder.

Then here came old Hoot Owl, charging in like a mad bull and roaring louder.

"You heathens!" he yelled. "You mad-dog hellions!"

He grabbed me by the shirt collar. He jerked me off little Clara and slung me down in the dirt. He broke a peeled chinaberry stick over Tim's head, then whirled to come at me again, waving the stub.

I guess if that rock hadn't been so handy to my reach I never would have done it. Or if old Hoot Owl hadn't crowded me after I'd done warned him, maybe I could have held off. But the rock was there, right under my fist when I hit the dirt. And I was scared and I was mad.

I came to my feet, with the feel of that rock in my hand making me plenty strong and plenty big. I drew it back for a throw and yelled at Hoot Owl, warning him.

"Keep coming at me with that stick, old man, and I'll let you have it!" I told him.

He was like all other grown-ups I know. He wouldn't listen. Not to me. He kept coming, so I let him have it. Just about the belly button. As hard as I could throw.

Well, it stopped him. Right in his tracks. With both hands grabbing at his paunch. With his big hoot-owl eyes bugged out of his head like a stepped-on frog's.

For about a second everybody was too surprised to let out a cheep. I thought to myself, *I guess that'll show 'em.*

Then Hoot Owl's knees began to buckle, and Illa Pratt let out a scream like a pig with its throat cut.

"Arliss Coates, you've killed him!"

That's when it came to me what a pickle I was in.

[21]

I didn't wait to see old Hoot Owl go down. I wheeled and took off toward the woods. Running as fast as I could run. Running and bawling again.

Not because I had killed old Hoot Owl. I knew better than that. You don't kill a grown man by hitting him in the belly with a rock. I'd chunked enough cows and pigs and mules to know that. But when you've been picked on till you've got to fight back, only you know you can't win and all you can do is run off into the woods somewhere, well you can get a feeling that'll scare the pants off anybody.

You're just so dang *lonesome*!

him with sharp sticks. When he finally quit rattling, I knew I'd killed him off. But I didn't have his rattles to prove it.

All evening I kept busy as a coon catching frogs, but when the sun slanted down till I judged it was time for school to let out, nothing had changed. I still had two lickings coming to me, maybe three. One from Papa for chunking them with rocks that morning. One from old Hoot Owl for knocking the wind out of him. And maybe another one from Papa when he learned that I'd gotten one from Hoot Owl.

Papa had warned me about that. "You get into trouble at school," he'd told me, "and you can expect worse when you get home."

And Papa would learn about it. You could bet on that. Some blabbermouth was bound to tell.

I'd sooner have eaten a plate of fried bats than to go home, but where else could I go? They had me trapped. Anywhere I went, they had me trapped.

Sure, I could go to lots of other places. Anybody in Salt Licks would take me in. Feed me, too, if I was hungry—and I was. Give me a bed to sleep in. And dry clothes if I was wet. But they'd also have to ask questions. They'd have to keep picking at me till they learned what the trouble was. Then they'd have to strike out for our cabin in a high lope to tell my folks where I was and what all I'd been up to.

When you're just a kid, grown-ups can get as pious as Moses about teaming up against you.

Anybody packing around worries as big as mine gets fuzzy brained as a Saturday-night drunk. He's as blind as a bullbat in bright sunlight. He's as deaf as a rotten stump in wet weather. He can walk right head-on into the worst kind of danger and never know it's there.

That's what happened to me when I came to the step-stone crossing on Birdsong Creek down below our cabin.

Across the creek, beside the spring where we got our drinking water, some people had made camp. There were two big sheet-covered wagons, with the harness laid back on the front wheels. There were womenfolks gathered around a cooking fire. There were grown men dragging up camp wood. There were horses and mules tied out under the trees, munching fodder and switching their tails at the flies. There were kids and dogs messing along the creek bank and grown-ups yelling at them not to fall in the water and drown.

On my side of the creek, right under my feet nearly, were more strangers. One was a bony-looking girl in a blue dress. One was a little old baby

[27]

boy, naked except for his diapers. They played in a patch of white creek sand shaded by the tall elm I stood under. A big rangy staghound lay in the sand beside them.

Well, there they all were, right out in the broad open. A bunch of strangers, camped at our spring. A sight to catch the eye of anybody not used to strangers.

But I didn't see them. And I didn't hear them. Not really. I was sweating too much blood. I was too busy churning my troubles around inside my skull.

I didn't even see the elm root that tripped and threw me when I started down the bank.

I did finally see the dog, after it was too late.

I heard his first warning snarl. That brought me alive enough to nearly die with a heart attack when he let out a sudden roar because I didn't stop.

I wanted to stop, the worst in the world. I knew that I had better stop, but I couldn't. I'd done lost my balance. I was done falling!

I landed on my hands and knees. He lunged for me, all hot eyes and red mouth and white teeth bared. I threw myself sideways, yelling with scare. But it didn't do any good. He nailed me by the throat and dragged me down into the sand.

For a couple of seconds there, I guess scare had a tighter grip on me than that old dog. I blacked

clear out. I didn't know one thing.

Then I heard a girl's voice, sharp with scolding. "Peabelly!" it said. "Turn him loose, Peabelly! You hear?"

I felt the sharp teeth clamping my throat give way and sucked in a long breath. Then I opened my eyes.

The girl had the dog gripped by a leather collar. She was dragging him off me. He still had his hackles raised. He was still hot eyed and snarling. Just to look at him gave me a shivering spell.

Back of the girl and the dog the baby sat in the sand. He looked fat and well fed. He stared at me out of big round blue eyes that were full of surprise. His mouth drooped at the corners. It was plain to see that he was fixing to cry if all this commotion didn't settle down pretty quick.

I felt about the same way.

I looked up at the girl. She was maybe nine years old. She had eyes as big and blue as the baby's. She had brown skin and teeth white as skim milk. She had a mop of shiny black hair that hung loose and ragged as the mane of a wild mule. She held to the dog and stared at me like I was some strange sort of varmint that she'd never set eyes on before.

"Who're you?" she wanted to know.

For a little bit I was so rattled I couldn't think who I was. That old dog had scared the wits out of me. I sat up and listened to my heart hammering blood against my eardrums. I felt my throat. It was all tight and achy. One place stung under the touch of my fingers. I guess that old dog's teeth has broken the hide there. Then, finally, I remembered.

"Me?" I said. "Why, I'm Arliss Coates. I live here. Who are you?"

"I'm Judy Sanders," she said. She pointed at the baby. "And that's Bubba. He's my little brother."

A man's voice called from across the creek, "Judy! What's a-going on over there?"

I looked across the creek. For the first time I saw the wagons and teams and people camped at our spring. The people were all standing and looking in our direction.

"Nothing to fret about, Uncle Nat," Judy called back. "It's just old Peabelly. He jumped this here boy."

"Hurt him?" Uncle Nat wanted to know.

I singled him out then. He was a tall, long-shanked man with a droop to his shoulders.

" 'Course not," Judy hollered at him. "Peabelly don't hurt nobody what don't hurt me and Bubba."

It riled me, her making so little of that old dog dragging me down.

I said, "How do you know I ain't hurt? How do you know I ain't tore all to pieces?"

"Well, you keep a watch on that old fool dog," Uncle Nat warned her.

"I'm keeping a watch on him," she yelled back.

"And he's keeping a watch on me and Bubba."

She turned then to me. "If Old Peabelly had aimed to hurt you," she said, "you'd done be dead. Old Peabelly, he'll kill you quicker than a bug. If he takes the notion."

I guessed she was right. I guessed that if the staghound had wanted, he could have done had my goozel turn out. I asked, "How come he jumped me?"

"He seen you threatening me and Bubba," she said. "The way you piled off down that bank, nearly right on top of us. And Peabelly, he won't let no harm come to me and Bubba. That's because we're orphants."

She spoke real proud, and bent to pat Peabelly on the head.

I looked at Peabelly and guessed that she was bragging some. But I understood. There was a time when Savage Sam had looked after me like that. When I was little. And there had been a dog before him that we called Old Yeller. He had saved me from a mad she-bear one time. When you've got dogs like that, you can't hardly keep from bragging on them.

I got up and brushed the sand off. "You mean you got no folks left?" I asked.

"Oh, we've got Uncle Nat and Aunt Cindy," she said, "and that whole passel of other shirttail relations you see yonder across the creek. They'll do to make out with. But it ain't the same as having folks of your own."

I started to ask what had killed off her papa and mama. Then I saw the start of tears in her eyes and held off. I guessed it was a sort of touchy matter with her.

I said, "What y'all doing camping at our spring?"

"Just laying over to let the teams rest," she said. "We're going out west."

"You ask Papa?"

"Your papa wasn't there, so we asked your mama. She let us."

Beside us Bubba cut loose with a giggling laugh. I looked at him. He held a fistful of sand above his head. He was spilling the sand down over his bare neck and shoulders. He was shivering like a body taken with the chills and laughing fit to choke.

"What's the matter with him?" I asked. "What's he doing that for?"

" 'Cause he likes to," Judy said. "The sand tickles his skin and makes him feel good. So he laughs."

I stood and watched Bubba for a minute. His shivering made me want to shiver. His laughing made me want to laugh with him. I didn't take much stock in babies, but I guessed I could come to like this little old knot-head.

[33]

Judy said, in a bothered voice, "Where's out west?"

"Why, I dunno," I said. "Just west of here, someplace, I guess."

"I wish it was here," she said. She looked all around. "I like it here. With all this pretty creek sand and the water and the shade trees and everything. Sure be nice if it was here."

"Well, I don't much guess it's here," I said. "Leastways, Papa don't never call this out west. He always talks like it is someplace farther on."

"That's how it's been ever since we left Missouri," she said. "It's always someplace farther on. I wish we could ever get there. I'm all worn out with waiting."

"Waiting for what?" I said.

"To get settled," she said. "So I can marry and have me and Bubba some folks of our own. Uncle Nat promised me I could. When we get settled."

"Married!" I said. "Are you crazy? You ain't big enough to get married."

"Maybe not right now," she said. "But Aunt Cindy says if I keep eating them out of house and home, like I'm doing, I'll soon be big as a skinned mule. I guess then I'll be big enough."

She stood gazing 'way off in the woods. Her eyes shone like maybe whatever she saw made her real happy.

I stared at her. I wondered how come the thinking of all females seemed to follow right down the same cow trail. I didn't know one yet who didn't have marrying on the brain by the time she could dress a Christmas doll.

I shook my head. I turned toward the stepping stones that led across the shallow water. I said, back over my shoulder, "You're bound to be crazy."

She didn't say anything.

Four

I WASN'T more than halfway across the creek when I had a stroke. What brought it on was the sight of Papa and the other horse hunters riding in to the Sanders' camp.

To let my heart settle down, I stopped and stood on a rock awhile. Getting dog-caught and swapping talk with the girl Judy had wiped my worries clean off my mind for a little bit. But now they came back, yapping at my heels again, louder than ever.

I tried to think what to do. Go take my licking now and get it over with? Or go hide out in the woods a little longer?

I noticed that the horses Papa and the others rode were all fagged out. They traveled with their heads hung low and their feet dragging out their tracks. Nobody was leading an extra horse, so I knew they hadn't caught the outlaw.

I listened to Papa howdying the settlers and making everybody acquainted all around. It gave me an idea. It wasn't one to build any great big hope on, but it was all the idea I had.

I knew Papa. He liked to visit with strangers. Maybe if I showed up now, he'd be so busy visiting that he'd forget all about the licking he owed me.

I decided to gamble on it. I braced myself with a deep breath and went on across the creek and up the bank to where they were all gathered around the wagons. I walked up, bold as a jaybird, like it never had come into my mind that Papa might want to whip me. Inside, though, I was as sneaky scared as a stray dog fixing to rob a meat house.

The others saw me coming but Papa didn't. He was down off his horse and talking like he couldn't wait to get it all said.

"I tell you it's sure fine country for settling," he was saying. "There on the south fork of the Rio Llano. Big pecan bottoms. Plenty of wild game for meat. Good grazing all over the hills. You'll be settling sort of on the edge of the desert, but with all them flowing springs you can irrigate. Seven hundred, I been told. Never bothered to make a count. But, like I say, you could have Indian trouble. Them Mescalero Apaches, they still raid that far down sometimes."

He turned then and saw me. His eyes lit up like the sight made him glad. He came and hugged me around the shoulders and shoved me to the front. He said, in a proud voice, "This here is my youngest boy, Arliss. He's little, but he's loud."

I'd felt warm and good inside when he put his arm across my shoulders. But that *little* business, it whetted on the edge. I jerked from under his arm.

"I done told you," I said, "that I ain't so *little*."

Papa looked surprised, then threw back his head for a big laugh. He spoke, confidential, to the settlers.

"Arliss generally carries his tail high and his stinger out. But me and his mama, we couldn't do without him."

The settlers all eyed me, like maybe I didn't amount to much. I had the same feeling about them. The men ran mostly to sloping shoulders, long face hair and tobacco-chewing. A good scrubbing with lye soap and hot water wouldn't have hurt the looks of the womenfolks.

The long-shanked man Judy called her Uncle Nat had one thing in common with Papa: he liked to talk. He nodded at me and said, "Howdy, boy," and made the campfire sizzle with a spurt of tobacco juice. Then he took up where Papa had left off.

"Well," he said, "I'll take my chances with the redskins. You can't hardly believe how them hogs stunk. Eating that rotten town garbage. Wallering in their own filth. Swarmed over by a black cloud of flies. And our shanty right downwind from the pen. We couldn't eat at our own table. Couldn't sleep in our own beds. All we could do was gag and throw up. Sicker than lizard-eating tomcats."

Papa said, "I take it that you ain't got much use for hogs."

"Then you take it wrong," Uncle Nat said. "I got respect enough for a hog. Give him room, and he'll live tolerably clean. What I can't stomach is the whickerbill who'll crowd a big bunch into a little pen, right up in a man's front door. In my opinion he rates lower than any hog."

"Couldn't you reason with him?" Papa wanted to know.

"*Reason* with him!" Uncle Nat jerked his head sideways, like a dog snapping at flies. "Man, did you ever try to reason with a hide-bound church deacon? And him down on the floor every night, rubbing sores on his knees, while he prays to the Almighty Dollar? I'd druther try to reason with a hog."

The longer he talked, the redder Uncle Nat got in the face. It was plain that his hog troubles were sure rubbing him on a raw place.

"What does he care," he kept on, "if I've sweated half a lifetime to buy that little old patch of ground and throw up a shanty to house my woman and younguns? That ain't his problem. His problem is to make another dollar. And if he has to raise a stink to do it, me and mine can live in the stink. We ain't collection-plate church deacons.

"You mean you just aim to let him go?" Wiley Crouch said.

"That's about the size of it," Sanderson said.

"Then what if I caught him?" Wiley wanted to know.

Sanderson grinned at Wiley. He knew that Wiley was running a bluff. He knew that Wiley had about as much chance of catching that outlaw horse as I did.

I had a sudden idea. "What about me?" I said. "What if I catch him? Is he my horse?"

I hadn't thought yet how I might catch him. I was too busy thinking how important I'd look if I did.

That's when they all laughed at me again. Papa and Sanderson and Travis and even the settlers. They all just haw-hawed at the very idea of me catching a horse that had gotten away from grown men.

It flew all over me. Just like it had that morning. I wanted to kill them.

"Dang it! I guess you think I *can't* catch him!" I yelled, suddenly mad enough to cry. I bent and grabbed up a couple of rocks off the ground.

"Look out!" Sanderson yelled. He threw both hands high over his head, making a big grinning show of giving up because he was afraid.

Papa's hand clamped down over my rock-throwing arm, gripping my wrist like a vise. He whirled me around to face him. His stare was plenty fierce and threatening.

"Arliss!" he said. "You drop them rocks!"

I dropped them. There wasn't anything else I could do.

"Now, you listen to me, young man," Papa went on. "Either you learn to halter that temper of yours or you're fixing to wind up with more trouble than you can handle with a tubful of rocks. You hear me?"

"Yes, sir," I said.

Sanderson blew out his breath with a big noise, like he'd just been shot at and missed. "Man alive!" he said, grinning all around. "Rubbing up against that Arliss is like touching a firebrand to a keg of gunpowder."

Everybody laughed. Papa turned me loose. I backed off, madder clean through. It shamed me, all of those people laughing at me like they were doing. But I guess I was lucky they were there. If they hadn't been there, Papa might have torn my tail-end worse than a wild sow's bed.

I almost wished he had. That way I'd have had one licking done and over with; one less to worry about.

I turned and headed for the house, careful not to look at anybody. Sanderson called after me.

"Tell you what, Arliss," he said. "Catch that old horse before Wiley does and he's yours. You can depend on that."

I kept going, like I didn't hear. I didn't have to look back to know that every dogged one of them was grinning like a briar-eating mule.

In a minute I heard footsteps close behind me, then a low voice asking, "You think you can catch him?"

I looked around but kept walking. It was Judy. She was hurrying to catch up with me. Her face showed that she had some understanding of how mad I was. Behind her I could see Bubba standing at the edge of the crowd with a hand on Peabelly's neck. Bubba's diapers were down around his feet.

"How would I catch him?" I asked.

"I think I know how," she said, "if you'll help."

"How?"

Between there and the house she told me. I listened, but I didn't pay her much mind. I was too full of the misery of being mad and getting laughed at.

At the yard gate she stopped and looked up at me, her eyes all eager and hopeful. Like maybe she thought I ought to brag on her.

That rubbed me wrong. Who did she think she was, to be smarter than me? I said, "That sounds just like the sort of harebrained idea you could expect a girl to come up with."

She flinched like I'd slapped her in the face.

All of a sudden, I felt tacky. She'd just been trying to help. I wished now that I hadn't been such a sorehead. But I didn't know how to tell her.

"But we could try it," she begged. "It wouldn't hurt none to try."

"Forget it," I said. "It won't work."

I pushed on through the gate. I left her standing there while I went on inside the cabin to see what Mama had for supper.

Five

BY morning I felt some different about Judy's idea.
I thought it just might *work*. And, like Judy said, it
wouldn't hurt to try. And what if it did work? What
if I came in, leading that old outlaw horse that the
grown-ups couldn't catch? I guessed that would
pop somebody's eyeballs.

It was Saturday. There was no school to bother
with. And maybe no licking to worry about before
Monday. I just might try it, I thought, if I could get
away from the house.

Without knowing it, Papa made that easy. At the
breakfast table, he said, "Arliss, I want you to saddle old Nellie and go bring in that pied cow and
her young calf that I seen yesterday. You ought to
find her in the first header draw this side of that
Onion Creek water hole. Her bag is all swelled up.
Liable to spoil if it ain't milked out."

He went on from there. He told just how to drive
the cow and calf. He warned me about running
her. She might get hot and mad and go on the fight.

He told me which would be the easiest ground to drive her over. He told me all the things he'd told me a thousand times about how to drive a cow but had to tell it again, because grown-ups don't ever think their younguns have got sense enough to come in out of the rain.

I just kept on eating and let him talk. I said "Yes, sir," in all the right places and didn't even start a fuss, like I generally did, about having to ride Nellie.

Nellie was a deadhead. You couldn't hardly spur her out of a trot. But for what I had in mind, an old pokey mare was just what I needed. A skittish horse would come quicker to a mare than he ever would to another horse.

Finally Papa got it all out of his system. He took a last couple of bites, then reached for his hat. He left the cabin like he had something that needed doing in a big hurry. I knew what it was. He had to get down to the settlers' camp. He needed to get an early start on a full day of talking.

I went out to the corrals and saddled Nellie. I got Papa's best roping rope and buckled it to the saddle. I hung a sack of ear-corn to the horn. I turned to lead Nellie out of the corral gate before mounting, and that's when I saw Judy and Bubba and Peabelly. They were all lined up, watching me through the gate.

Judy's face was full of excitement. "You're fixing to try it!" she said.

I hedged. "I'm fixing," I said, "to go bring in a cow with a young calf."

"But you're going to try it," she said again. "I can tell. You've got a rope—and you've got the corn."

"All right," I said. "Maybe I'll give it a try. If I get enough time."

She looked at me like she expected me to give her something. I didn't know what. When she couldn't hold it any longer, she told me.

"I want to go, too!" she said. "Can I go? I want to see if it'll work."

I might have known what was coming.

"Girls talk too much," I said. "Out in the woods, they keep right on chattering. Scare everything off."

"I won't say a word," she said. "I'll promise to keep quiet as a mouse."

"You'd be the first one," I said. "And what about Bubba? Who'll look after him with you gone?"

"Peabelly will look after Bubba," she said. "He won't let nothing harm him. He knows we're or-phants."

She waited, looking hopeful.

That sort of got to me. Her being an orphan and so anxious and just asking, instead of raising a fuss, like maybe she had a right to go.

[49]

I let her wait while I studied on it. I let her wait long enough to get the idea that I didn't *have* to take her. I'd done heard Papa say that the only way to handle a female is to take the upper hand and keep it.

Finally, I said, "All right. If you'll keep your mouth shut."

Her eyes lit up like I'd handed her a Christmas present. "I'll go tell Uncle Nat," she said.

She whirled around and headed for the camp, dragging Bubba along by one hand.

"Just tell him we're cow-hunting," I warned.

"I won't be but a minute," she called back.

She broke into a run, dragging Bubba along so fast that he lost his diapers. They didn't trip him, though, and she didn't notice, and Peabelly came along and picked them up and went loping along behind, packing them in his mouth.

We rode out into the hills. Fall was in the air and this early in the morning the hills were all smoky. Judy rode behind, holding to saddle strings with each hand. Cow trails followed the easy ground through the brush and rocks. Every little piece the trails forked and wound off in different directions. I kept Nellie at a jog-trot, following whichever trail came the closest to leading toward the Onion Creek water hole.

We had about an hour's ride ahead of us. Long

before it was over I learned how stupid I was to bring Judy along on a wild-horse hunt. It wasn't that she talked so much. It was just that she was so ignorant and I had to keep explaining things to her.

She saw coon tracks in the sandy trails and thought they were baby tracks. She didn't know that a green mountain boomer lizard could stand up and run on his hind feet. I had to show her that when a chaparral bird starts leading a rider down a trail he always keeps the same distance ahead, no matter if you walk or run a horse. She'd never seen how the sensitive briar vine folds up its leaves when you brush them with your hand. She didn't know that the yellow-flowering compass plant always points its leaves north and south. She'd never seen a deer scrape till I showed her the worn side of a cedar tree where some old buck had rubbed the velvet from his horns. She'd never tasted the sweet of mesquite beans or eaten a prickly-pear apple or heard tell of using the leaves of a tickle-tongue bush to stop your bleeding. A body just couldn't hardly believe all the things she didn't know.

By the time we found the cow with the young calf I was worn to a frazzle. I couldn't hardly talk above a whisper.

"Now, look," I told her, "this jabbering's got to stop. We ride in to that water hole with all this chatter going on, we're never gonna see hide nor hair of that old horse."

"I won't say another word," she said, and she didn't.

We rounded a bend in the creek and came to the water hole. It was a clear pool at the foot of a rocky ledge. It had cattails growing at the lower end. On the side away from the ledge, out apiece from the water, stood a live oak mott.

We rode toward the mott. Red-winged blackbirds flew up out of the cattails, all excited about us. They screamed and circled above our heads, then settled back into the cattails after we passed on. A gray fox quit the water and went up over the ledge. He took to the brush on a bent-tail run.

One live oak stood away from the others. It was bigger and stooping and had one long branch reaching out for the water. I sized it up. It looked like the sort of tree I wanted.

I reined Nellie to a stop under this stooping live oak. We got down. I tied Nellie to the tree and stripped off the saddle gear. I shook the ear-corn out of the sack for Nellie to eat on. I dragged the saddle away and hid it in the mott. I brought the rope back with me. I gave Judy a hand-up into the tree, then climbed after her. We worked our way along the far-reaching branch till we found good places to sit. I tied one end of the rope to the branch we sat on and ran me out a loop about the

[53]

right size to catch a horse. Then we settled down to wait.

Like I'd expected, it was a long wait. It seemed longer, I guess, because we had to sit so still. And we couldn't talk. And we couldn't know for sure that our wait wouldn't be wasted. I'd seen horse tracks at the edge of the water as we rode in, but that didn't have to mean anything. After the chase Papa and them had given him yesterday, that old horse might have quit the country for good.

I looked up at the sun. It was maybe nine o'clock. I didn't much expect that horse to show up before noon. If he came. And if he came, he still might get wind of me and Judy and shy off. Or maybe never come within reach of my loop. A body just couldn't tell. All we could do was sit quiet and watch and listen. But all the time I kept thinking: *Wouldn't it be something if I did happen to catch that old horse?*

Take a country like ours, where the water holes are far apart, a body can hide himself and get to see a real show, just watching what comes in to drink or what comes to catch meat. And you don't have to hide yourself much. In fact, you can sit right out in the broad open and see plenty. Sight of you doesn't mean much to most wild things. They generally can't tell you from a rock or a stump—if you won't move or make any racket and if they don't get wind of you. Getting wind of you is the worst;

and you can't hardly keep them from it, if you don't know what direction they're coming from.

Of course, a wild turkey, he can't smell you, but he makes up the difference by having an eye that'll nail you down in a hurry. Anytime you want a wild turkey to come in your direction you sure better freeze solid.

Other than a bunch of little old birds, coming and going all the time, it was wild turkeys that showed up first. I saw them come sneaking out of the brush. There were two old hens with a late brood of maybe a dozen young ones. The young ones were about the size of bantam chickens. They weren't scary, but the old ones were. The old ones could hear Nellie eating corn. It was a strange sound to them, and they didn't trust it.

The old hens had lots of stretch to their necks and they kept craning their heads around this way and that, trying to make out what they could hear. The little ones kept trying to hurry on to the water, but the old hens couldn't take more than two or three steps without having to stop and let out a low *put-put* warning. Then all the young ones would stop and stretch their necks and try to see, too.

Finally, they got close enough to see Nellie. She didn't look like much of a threat to them, but they were still suspicious. And they had a right to be. For down next to the water, waiting between the pads of a low-growing prickly pear, was a weasel.

came, prancing down off that rocky slant, as sure-footed as a cat. All horse from the ground up, with just one thing to hurt his looks. That was the number of brands he wore.

They ranged from his jawbone back to the root of his tail. They were all shapes and all sizes. They marked him for what he was—an outlaw. There was no other excuse for that fine a horse to have changed owners so many times.

Below us, Nellie was having wall-eyed fits. She was nickering, wringing her tail, slinging her head from side to side, now and then lunging out to the end of her tie-rope, hoping to pull loose.

I paid Nellie no mind. She was just the bait. I kept my eye on the outlaw horse she was helping to bring into the trap. I sat gripping my loop, which was spread out on the branches behind me. I kept thinking: *You big pretty devil. You ever come within reach of my loop, you're fixing to wear still another brand!*

He came racing across the shallow edge of the pool, knocking sheets of water high in the sunlight. He came pounding on up the bank, his hammering hoofs chopping up chunks of mud and slinging them behind him. The way he kept on coming it looked for a second like he would charge right on in without stopping.

Then, all of a sudden, he snorted and set his hoofs down hard. He braced with all four feet, plowing furrows in the loose sand that the creek had thrown up at flood time. He slid to a halt. He stood head high and whistling, stomping the ground with his forefeet.

I nearly died. There he was, just outside the reach of my rope. Scary now. Suspicious of some scent or sound that didn't set right with him.

He wasn't seeing me and Judy. He wasn't looking up at us. He had his eye on Nellie. But something was holding him back.

Would he come on in? The way I felt, he nearly had to. But would he?

Up to this time I'd wanted to catch him, just to show Papa and the others that I could. Now I wanted *him*—for *me*. I wanted him so bad that I could nearly taste it. But would he ever come in reach?

He finally did. It took him a while. He had to snort and nicker again. He had to sling his mane and wave his tail in the air. He had to romp around a little. Then, here he came, sidling right up to the whickering Nellie. Paying no mind to how her ears were laid back and her teeth all bared.

All in one quick move, I stood up on the limb and whipped my loop into the air over my head.

He saw me then. He wheeled, blasting the air with a loud snort. But it was done too late. I had him within reach. I swung my loop down and set it up in the air ahead of him. It opened and at just exactly the right time. He ran square into it, and I jerked up the slack.

"I got him!" I yelled.

I dropped the rest of the rope. I grabbed for a handhold on an upstanding limb. That didn't do much good. He hit the end of that rope, running like the dogs were after him.

Which was too much for that old doty tree limb we sat on. He jerked it right out from under me and Judy. He tore it clear loose from the main tree trunk. It crashed to the ground. Me and Judy piled up right beside it, with Judy screaming her head off.

I let her scream. I jumped to my feet and took off after the horse. But it turned out there wasn't any need to chase him. He just dragged that tree branch a little piece while the scare was still on him. After that he wheeled about and stood facing me, stomping his forefeet and whistling loud. But he wasn't fighting that rope, not even a little bit. Somebody had already broken him of that.

I took my time then. I circled the tree branch and went toward him, walking slow and easy. I went to sweet-talking him, like I'd heard Papa and Burn Sanderson do when they set out to gentle a wild one.

I said, "All right, old boy, you just well settle down and take your medicine, 'cause you're done caught, done outfigured and outsmarted by me,

[60]

Arliss Coates. I got my rope on you when the others couldn't. They laughed at the idea of a boy catching you when grown-ups couldn't, but you see who done it. I guess they'll get to laugh awhile out of the other side of their mouths now."

I'd heard Burn Sanderson say that when it comes to sweet-talking a skittish horse or a female the words you say don't count for half as much as the tone of voice you use.

I kept talking till I got my hands on the rope. I gave it a little tug. The outlaw palomino came toward me. He rolled his eyes and snorted a little, but he came right on up till I could put my hand on his nose.

I looked around at Judy. She was coming toward me, all big-eyed and holding her breath, like she couldn't believe what she saw. But I guessed she could believe that I knew how to sweet-talk a horse.

She came on up, still staring at the horse, then said "Ummmmm!" like a body will do sometimes when they bite into an extra-sweet plum. "Ain't he the prettiest thing!"

"He's sure a dandy, all right," I agreed.

She frowned. "But ain't it a shame that you can't ride him?"

"Who says I can't ride him?" I said. "I caught him, didn't I? And he's been rode."

Up to then I hadn't thought about riding him. I'd

been too busy catching him. But telling me I couldn't do something always did rub me wrong. I'd been told that too many times.

"But he's an outlaw, Arliss," she argued. "He's so big and so strong and—"

She turned and looked at me, without finishing, and all of a sudden I was fighting mad again.

"And I guess you think I'm too little!" I said. "I guess you think I'm a-scared of him!"

"Oh, no, Arliss," she said. "I didn't mean that. I just meant that he might hurt you bad. Or maybe kill you."

That just made me all the madder. "Well, I'll tell you one thing," I said. "If I didn't have a frazzled-out girth on my saddle, I'd just show you if I'm scared of him or not."

She looked at me and then at the horse and then back at me again. "I don't guess," she said, "that your papa would have a good strong girth back at the house, would he?"

Six

ONE time I swallowed a couple of live minnows—
to win a pocketknife off Scab Haley—and it is hard
to tell what a cold, fluttery feeling I had inside my
stomach before those minnows quit flopping
around and finally settled down to die.

Anyhow, that's the sort of feeling I had to deal
with by the time we reached the corrals back at the
house. Only, this time, it felt more like I'd swallowed a whole bait bucket full of minnows.

Not that I was scared, you understand. I'd done
made up my mind about that. I aimed to show Judy
Sanders that I wasn't the least bit scared. I aimed
to show Papa, too, and Mama, and anybody else
who held the fool notion that I wasn't big enough
to crawl the hump of this outlaw horse and ride the
kinks out of him.

But I did wish the feeling of live minnows inside
my stomach would settle down.

We drove the cow and calf to within a hundred
yards of the cabin and left them in the brush. Then

[64]

we led Salty into the corrals through the back gate, where the corncrib would hide us from the settler camp down at the spring.

Papa was still down there; and, once, he could have seen us, only he was too wrapped up in some tall tale he was telling. I knew this by the way he kept waving both hands in the air, busier than a Mexican describing a bear fight.

I stripped my saddle gear off Nellie and laid it on the ground. I led the outlaw to the snubbing post and tied his head down low, for easier bridling. Then I unbuckled the frazzled-out girth from my saddle and went to get Papa's.

Papa's saddle hung under a shed next to the corncrib. Beside it hung a pair of big old Chihua-hua spurs that Burn Sanderson had given Papa. They had sharp-spiked rowels about four inches across and felt like they'd weigh five pounds apiece. Sanderson said he'd taken them off a cow thief he and some other Rangers had shot down around Uvalde last spring. Sanderson wouldn't wear them, claiming they were horse killers, and Papa wouldn't wear them for the same reason. But the thought hit me that with the ride I was fixing to make, a pair of horse-killer spurs might come in real handy. So I buckled them on and went drag-ging them through the corral dust to where I put Papa's girth on my saddle.

Salty took the bits between his teeth without any

fight. He stood quiet while I let out the headstall to fit his long jaws. He didn't flinch when I laid the blanket across his back or hump up the least bit when I set my saddle on him. But the rascal was laying for me. That was plain from the way he kept cutting his eyes around till the whites showed. He was just waiting for me to make a wrong move and give him the advantage. Then he'd open up a bag of tricks calculated to show who was boss.

I stopped him cold with his first trick. That was when I drew up on the cinch and he started swelling. The harder I pulled on the latigo strap, the bigger his belly got. This was so I couldn't set my saddle down tight enough on his back to keep it from slipping when he let the air out.

Well, I'd seen "blowers" before. I'd seen how Papa and Burn Sanderson handled them. So I took a good grip on the strap and leaned my full weight against it. Then I kicked the horse in the belly and jerked as hard as I could.

That kick knocked the wind out of him. He grunted and snorted and wheeled away from me. But he was too late. I'd done yanked that cinch up tighter than Papa ever laced Mama into her Sunday corset.

I let him consider that awhile, then untied the rope from the snubbing post and slipped the loop over his head. I reached to pull the reins through the loop, and that's when he tried to bite me. I jerked my hand away, just in time, and busted him on the nose with my fist. He fell back then, squealing. He reared high and went to trying to chop my brains out with his forefeet. I stepped out of his reach and hauled down on the reins. When he came back to the ground, I gave him a second hard kick in the belly.

Behind me, Judy sucked in a loud breath. "Oh, gee, Arliss!" she said. "I'm scared!"

"Well, keep out of the way," I told her.

"I mean for you," she said. "He's so big and so mean. I'm scared he'll kill you."

I wished that she would hush.

"He's big and he's mean," I said, "but he ain't killed me yet."

I stuffed in my shirttail. I pulled up my britches and tightened my belt a notch. I yanked my hat down on my head and took a deep breath. Then I lifted a foot to set it in a stirrup that hung so high off the ground I could just barely reach it. I caught hold of the saddlehorn to help pull myself up—and suddenly felt that batch of cold minnows in my stomach taking off in all directions. Like maybe a killer gar had hit among them.

Right then I knew that I didn't want up in that saddle. I didn't want up there, even a little bit. Not with it setting on the back of a bad horse that now looked at least nineteen feet tall.

I don't guess I'd have ever made it, if it hadn't

been for Mama. She picked this time to come racing around the corner of the cabin, screaming her head off.

"No, Arliss. No! Don't you get on that horse!"

Well, there it was again. Somebody yelling at me not to do something. Just the same as saying I was too *little* to do it.

I gritted my teeth. I went up and across the saddle, quick as a cat. I was mad clear through. Too mad to be scared anymore. Too mad to care what that outlaw horse might do. I just rocked back in my saddle and slammed the rowels of those big Chihuahua spurs into old Salty's shoulders.

What happened next was like setting off a batch of dynamite under a mesquite stump. Salty let out a bawl you could have heard a mile off. He reared straight up. He rose so high it looked like he aimed to come back over on top of me.

But I was laying for him, just like he'd been laying for me. I swapped ends with my quirt and whacked the loaded butt of it down between his ears as hard as I could hit.

I must have struck a nerve, for he dropped like he'd been shot. He went to his knees, and I thought he was going clear on down. Then up he lunged again, in a weaving, high-rolling twist that rattled every leather on my saddle and came mighty close to snapping me loose from it.

He hit the ground with a jolt that shot a stab of

pain up my backbone. Then he bogged head and tail and went after it in earnest, bawling and pitching and slamming sideways into the corral poles and swapping ends and taking off in some other direction.

Squawking chickens flew every whichway. Ducks quacked. Geese honked. Turkeys gobbled. Judy screamed. Mama screamed. Nellie squealed and tried to jump the corral fence and couldn't and fell flat on her back, right under us. Savage Sam came charging into the corral bawling his mightiest. From down at the settlers camp came a lot of hollering and yelling.

All of this hullaballoo, I just sort of half heard and half saw. I sure didn't pay it any mind. I didn't have time. I was too busy clawing for handholds. I was hurting too bad from the beating that saddle was giving my tailbone. I was too scared of that grunting, coughing bawl Salty let out every time his feet popped the hardpan.

That bawling! It was enough to scare you blind. It sounded worse than the squall of a wounded panther when he springs. It told me, right from the start, that I had to stay in that saddle. No matter how that outlaw rocked and weaved and twisted and rolled under me, I still had to stay with what I had. If that old horse ever shook me loose, he'd stomp me to death the second I hit the ground.

So I stayed.

[69]

I can't exactly tell you how, and it sure wasn't any brag ride. Because I was all over that outlaw horse, sometimes behind the saddle, sometimes in front of it, and plenty of times down off one side or the other. But for every bone-jarring jump he made, I made a quicker move, clawing for mane and any scrap of leather I could get my hands on and wishing I could sprout more hands.

So, when finally he did throw up his tail and call it quits, I was still up in the middle of him. My brain was fuzzy. My nose was leaky. My head roared, and every bone in my body felt like it had been yanked out of socket. But no matter; I was still up in the big middle of him.

For a little bit I was too stunned to move. Or too surprised. Or too scared. Anyhow, I just sat quiet in the saddle and watched Papa fling open the corral gate and come charging through.

Right on Papa's heels came Mama and she was crying. And behind Mama came Burn Sanderson and Bud Searcy and Wiley Crouch on fast-running horses, cutting in ahead of the straggled-out settler bunch hurrying up from the creek. And the whole kit and kaboodle of them—from Papa clear on back to the last waddling, fat Sanders woman— looked as wild-eyed as range cattle hightailing for the brush when the heel flies hit them.

With my wits still so scattered, it didn't make sense to me right then—everybody's rushing in on

loud laugh that lasted till the tears came.

"Arliss Coates," he said. "If you ain't a ring-tailed tooter, I never saw one."

Judy's Uncle Nat held a sober face and shook his head, frowning. He said, "A man just can't hardly believe it. A little old feller like that, making such a ride."

"That's because he's a cowboy," Judy put in.

It seemed like the ground didn't want to hold steady under my feet, so I put a hand out and caught hold of my saddle stirrup.

"I ain't so *little*," I told Judy's Uncle Nat.

Sanderson laughed louder.

Wiley Crouch said in a sneering voice, "Aw, just an accident. Likely, that old horse wouldn't pitch, like if he had a man astraddle of him."

Old man Searcy bristled up. "Accident, my big foot!" he argued. "What was I telling you fellers yesterday? Wasn't I saying that, when it comes to topping out the bad ones, your little short-coupled fellers has got the edge on the rest of us. Their center of gravity hangs lower. Didn't I never tell you about that kid horse-breaker down on the Río Frío? Short-coupled as Little Arliss, here. Wasn't a lot older."

I cut in on Searcy, to ask Sanderson again, "Didn't you say I could have him if I caught him?"

Sanderson sobered suddenly. He frowned and looked uneasy. He studied awhile, then said in a quiet voice, "That's what I said, Arliss. But, son, you don't want that horse."

"Don't want him," I said. "What makes you think I don't want him?"

"But, Arliss!" Mama put in. "He's too danger-ous!"

A sort of far-off sounding roar started up inside my head.

Papa said, "It don't matter what you want or what Sanderson said. You don't get that horse. He's a killer."

"He'll hurt you, son," Sanderson said. "He's done hurt you, for that matter, and he'll hurt you worse."

I felt a big mad boiling up inside me. Here it was again. All of them, ganging me, fixing to cheat me out of my rights.

Tears, hot as gnats, stung my eyes. The roaring sound got louder. I dragged a shirt sleeve across my leaky nose, and it came away all bloody. I yelled at Sanderson.

"Who says I'm hurt?"

Mama saw the blood and screamed at the top of her voice, "Oh, Arliss!"

I backed off and sidestepped her, moving toward a litter of fist-sized rocks lying in the corral dust. Just let me get my hands on those rocks, and I'd show them a thing or two about cheating me out of my rights.

[75]

I was so mad I was crying now. I yelled back over my shoulder, "I know how it is. I can catch him when y'all can't. I can ride him when y'all can't. But I still can't have him. Because I'm too *little!*"

I bent down, reaching for a couple of rocks. The roar inside my skull swelled to a sudden WHOOM!

At the same time, the ground tilted up and slammed me in the face, knocking me colder than a steel wedge.

Seven

I CAME to, with my insides on fire, clear down to my toenails, it seemed like. I was choking and coughing and gagging and strangling. I was fighting out with both fists at all the hands holding me down.

When, finally, I caught my breath, I yelled, "Turn me loose, dang it!" and heard Papa say, "Good!" and somebody sat me up. My sight cleared then and I found myself sitting on the kitchen table, ringed around by a crowd of wide-eyed people. Backing off from me was old man Searcy, clutching a whisky jug to his belly and looking real proud of himself.

"Like I say," he said, grinning all around, "what ailment good corn whisky won't cure ain't worth the trouble to have in the first place."

I knew then that it was whisky burning my insides and I got dizzy sick and tried to puke, but nothing came up.

Mama came with a wet rag and washed my face

and hugged me up and fussed at Papa.

"It just don't seem right," she told Papa, "to pour all that nasty whisky down a poor little old hurt boy."

"It brought him around," Burn Sanderson pointed out.

"And," Papa added, "it won't keep his bowels torn up for a solid week, like that mullein-weed tea you were fixing to give him."

"But," Mama argued, "the preacher says—"

Old man Searcy cut in with a snort. "Preachers," he declared, "can find sin in a pot full of beans. If the beans taste good."

I slipped down off the table and tried to stand, but suddenly the kitchen and all the people in it went to spinning around me. I grabbed at the table for support but missed it, and Papa caught me up before I fell. He lifted me in his arms and, this time, when I tried to puke, I nearly turned wrong-side-out all over the kitchen floor.

A bunch of the womenfolks gasped and said "Oh, my goodness!" and "How awful" and things like that, but all Papa said was, "Any blood in it, Burn?" Burn Sanderson said, "Not a bit," and Papa said, "Good! That means there ain't nothing tore loose inside him!" and old man Searcy said, "All he needs now is to sleep off that drink and he'll be fit as a fiddle again."

So Papa carried me out of the kitchen and across

the dog run to the other part of the cabin, where he dumped me in bed. And Mama, she came at me with that wet rag again and went to washing my face, and that's the last I remember until about bullbat time that evening, when Judy Sanders came inside the room leading her Uncle Nat by the hand.

She pushed past Papa and Mama and Burn Sanderson and old man Searcy, who were all sitting around, talking quiet and wearing sober looks, like grown people have a habit of doing when they're sitting up with the sick. She pointed a finger at me and said, "He's the one, Uncle Nat!"

"For what, Honey?" her Uncle Nat asked.

"For marrying," she said.

"For marrying?" he said. He gave her a puzzled look. "I reckon I don't quite understand."

She said, "Didn't you make me a promise that when we got out west I could marry a cowboy and have folks of my own?"

The face of her Uncle Nat took on the look of a body who feels like he's getting hemmed up in a corner.

I began to get the same feeling.

"Well, yes, Honey," her Uncle Nat said, "but—"

"Well, he's a real cowboy," Judy cut in. "He caught that old outlaw horse that nobody else could catch—and rode him, too. So he's the one I want."

[79]

Burn Sanderson's big laugh boomed out. Papa's face split in a wide grin. I jerked up and sat in bed. My head was still woozy and I ached all over, like I'd been beaten with a club, but worst of all was that sudden feeling inside me that I was about to fall into a trap.

I said to Judy, "You gone crazy?"

She just glanced at me, but didn't answer, then turned to wait with an anxious look on her face, while her Uncle Nat's eyes went begging for help from one grown-up to the next. Finally, he said, "Well, Honey, you've got me sort of stumped. Now, Arliss here, he's a fine little feller and a real cowboy, just like you say. But when it comes to marrying—well, it don't look to me like he's hardly marrying size as of now—nor you, either, for that matter."

Judy's bottom lip went to quivering. "You mean," she said, "that I can't have him? But you promised!"

Her Uncle Nat dragged a red handkerchief from his hip pocket and wiped the sweat from his face. "I know, Honey," he said. "But look. Let's consider for a minute."

Judy's blue eyes went to blaming him. "You mean," she said, "that you were lying to me. Just like Arliss' folks were lying to him, when they promised him that horse he caught, then gave it away to somebody else?"

That one shook me. I stared at her while she stared up at her uncle, like she couldn't believe what she'd heard. Then her face fell all to pieces and she turned and went running out of the cabin, bawling her head off.

"All I ever wanted," she cried, "was just some folks of my own."

I could have felt sorry for her, if she hadn't been so crazy in the head.

Mama jumped up out of her chair, saying "Bless her poor little old broken heart!" and went chasing off after Judy.

I sat quiet for a minute, looking from Papa to Burn Sanderson to old man Searcy. They had all hushed their laughing now, and every one of them shied off from meeting my eyes. A pack of sheep-killing dogs wouldn't have looked any more guilty.

I finally asked, "Who's got my horse?"

Papa flared up. "Now, Arliss," he said, "I done told you that you can't have that horse."

"I let Wiley Crouch have him," Burn Sanderson said. "I thought it best."

"It's safer, that way, boy," Searcy said.

Then they lit in on me, all of them, telling me all over again what a bad horse that outlaw was, how he was too dangerous for a little old boy to ride, how he'd done killed one man and crippled a dozen others, how they'd pick me as fine a saddle horse as a body could want out of that Brad Tulley bunch of horses that Burn Sanderson has just bought.

I lay back in bed and let them pile it on, thick. And I didn't argue. There wasn't any use. They had me whipped—for now. I was too puny to fight back. But, I told myself, if they thought they had me whipped for good, they didn't have any more sense than a pack of hounds trying to dig a badger out of a hole.

Just let me get on my feet again. I'd show them!

ABOUT THE AUTHOR

Fred Gipson's *OLD YELLER* and *SAVAGE SAM* continue to have enormous popularity today for children everywhere. *OLD YELLER* has won numerous awards and was the basis for the well-known Walt Disney movie of the same title.

Born in 1908, Mr. Gipson grew up in the Texas hill country about which he wrote with affection and verve. After working as a reporter for newspapers in Texas and Colorado, he started free-lance writing in 1940. While managing a small stock farm near Mason, Texas, he wrote books for both children and adults, among them *THE HOME PLACE, THE TRAIL-DRIVING ROOSTER, HOUND-DOG MAN,* and *RECOLLECTION CREEK.*

Fred Gipson died in August of 1973.